MARATHON MASTER

True HORSE Stories

MARATHON MASTER

BY JUDY ANDREKSON

Illustrations by David Parkins

Tundra Books

Published in Canada by Tundra Books,
75 Sherbourne Street, Toronto, Ontario M5A 2P9

Published in the United States by Tundra Books of Northern New York,
P.O. Box 1030, Plattsburgh, New York 12901

Library of Congress Control Number: 2007906498

Library and Archives Canada Cataloguing in Publication

Andrekson, Judy
Fosta : marathon master / Judy Andrekson ;
illustrated by David Parkins.

(True horse stories)
ISBN 978-0-88776-838-5

1. Kintamani Fosta (Horse) – Juvenile literature. 2. Endurance horses – Australia – Biography – Juvenile literature. 3. Arabian horse – Australia – Biography. I. Parkins, David II. Title. III. Series.

SF355.K55A54 2008 j798.2'40929 C2007-905365-3

We acknowledge the financial support of the Government of Canada through the Book Publishing Industry Development Program (BPIDP) and that of the Government of Ontario through the Ontario Media Development Corporation's Ontario Book Initiative. We further acknowledge the support of the Canada Council for the Arts and the Ontario Arts Council for our publishing program.

Design: Terri Nimmo

ONTARIO ARTS COUNCIL
CONSEIL DES ARTS DE L'ONTARIO

Tundra Books and the author thank Silver Maple Farm Inc., **www.smfarabs.com**, for their enthusiasm and kind permission to use the cover photo of their beautiful horse, Rebel Rose, taken by Stuart Vesty.

Printed and bound in Canada

This book is printed on acid-free paper that is 100% recycled, ancient-forest friendly (40% post-consumer recycled).

1 2 3 4 5 6 13 12 11 10 09 08

Acknowledgments

I would like to express my deepest thanks to the following people who provided so much invaluable information while I researched this story.

Ieva Peters, Ross Mudie, and Indy Rosser, who put out the call for "horses with a Shahzada story" in the first place, helped me locate the Lindsays, and provided information about the Shahzada as I went along. Thank you so much. You got the ball rolling!

Susan Walker, John Robertson, Helen Brown, and Lou McCormack, thank you for sharing your stories of Fosta with me. It was so great to hear from the people whose lives were touched by this remarkable little horse.

A very special, heartfelt thanks to Tom Perkins, one of Australia's most enthusiastic endurance promoters, and a deep well of information and insight. I appreciate everything you offered – the trail maps, the photos, the advice – and, yes, hopefully I can take you up on that old

[illegible] Shahzada for myself.

had the chance to get to know [illegible]

well as I have.

I also want to thank everyone I spoke to who corrected me, scolded me, and insisted I get it right, whenever I asked about endurance *racing* rather than endurance *tests* or *rides.* To Finish is to Win – I got it!!!

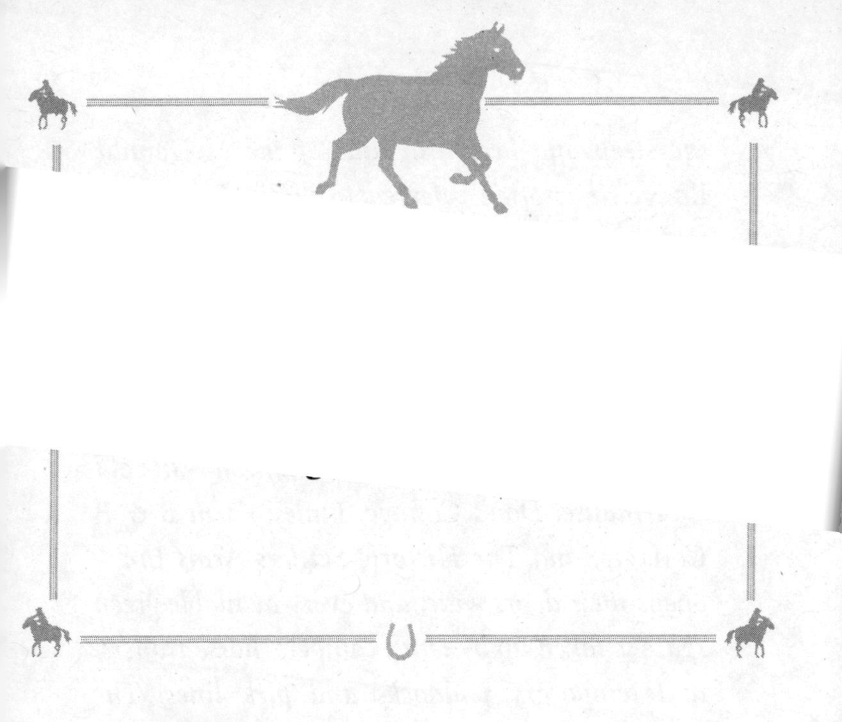

Endurance News – August, 1998
17th Annual Shahzada – Breaking Records

For fifty-one weeks of each year, the tiny village of St. Albans lies quiet and peaceful. Its residents, numbering around two hundred people, enjoy a friendly, rural existence. Located about two hours northwest of Sydney, Australia, the village is nestled in the narrow McDonald River Valley, surrounded by the steep and beautiful hills of the McDonald Range. It is often referred to as the Forgotten Valley, *as it has been bypassed by all major roads and railways, and a trip to St. Albans feels like walking a half-century back in time.*

But once a year, during the last full week of August, the town swells to around a thousand people. Every available accommodation – the old Courthouse, Don's Cottage, Linley Farm B & B Cottages, and The Historic Settlers Arms Inn – opens their doors wide, and every available green space is taken up by tents, campers, horse trailers, and temporary paddocks and pick lines. The general store / restaurant / souvenir shop-in-one does the best business it sees all year, and the pub is full with locals and visitors alike. For this one week, St. Albans comes to life – and all for the sake of a horse race.

The race – or rather, the ride or test, as it is more correctly known in endurance circles (endurance riders are pretty touchy about this term as there is a great deal of negativity surrounding horse racing and they like to keep their sport strictly separate) – is the Shahzada.

Known as the Ultimate Endurance Test, *the* [illegible] *is the only event of its length in Australia,* [illegible] *in the*

[illegible]

horse-and [illegible] *ones that enter each year. The buckle* [illegible] *completing this grueling, five-day, four-hundred-kilometer test is one of the most sought after awards by Australian endurance riders, along with riders from several other nations.*

This year's Shahzada promises to be even more exciting than usual, as two horses strive to break amazing records and make their mark as outstanding endurance competitors.

Robert Ward, on his incredibly tough and fast horse, Hawksbury Impala, is looking to finish in first place for the third straight year and hopes to better his own speed record of 25.18 hours, set just last year.

Alan Lindsay and his remarkable gelding, Kintamani Fosta, are looking to break a record of their own. Completion of this year's Shahzada will mark the tenth time the diminutive bay has survived the rigors of the challenging course out of eleven attempts, toppling the record now held by Gilgelad (10/12), and marking Fosta as one of the most consistent and enduring horses the test has ever produced.

Four hundred kilometers of rugged terrain is a lot to ask of an eighteen-year-old horse, especially one who hasn't raced in close to a year. The endurance motto "To Finish is to Win" (a particularly relevant motto in the Shahzada, where over a hundred horses enter the ride annually, but often less than half finish) will have a whole new meaning at this year's event.

To complete the Shahzada is to realize a dream, and as with all horse sports, that dream begins with a foal. . . .

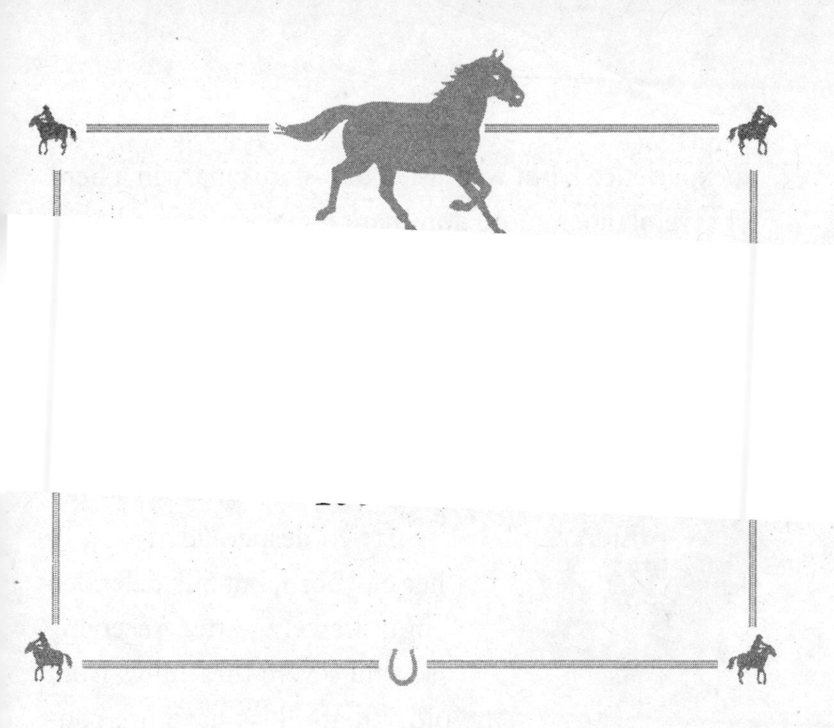

It was two days before Christmas, 1980, when the little bay colt arrived at Kintamani Stud. He arrived quietly and unexpectedly, some time during the warm summer night, but by the time he was discovered early the next morning, there was major trouble.

His dam, a little Australian Stock Horse, was an inexperienced, first-time mother. She had shown no signs of the impending foaling the evening before, and had been left in the broodmare pasture with the other heavy-bellied mares. Malpa's River Lisa was not only small and inexperienced, but was also a low-status mare in a herd of several older, more dominant females.

Another mare, also near her foaling date, became maternal at the sight of Lisa's newborn foal. Silk claimed the colt as her own, and chased Lisa away from him before the pair had a chance to bond. The young mother tried desperately to get to her newborn, but Silk defended him fiercely. After receiving several severe thrashings from the older mare, Lisa gave up, confused and exhausted.

Alan Lindsay was, not surprisingly, quite confused at first when he saw Silk with the colt at her side the next morning. Silk's sides still bulged with her own unborn foal, and yet she looked as though she had fully bonded with this one. Then Alan spotted Lisa, caked with dried sweat and dust, fresh teeth marks raked across her rump and neck, a full bag of milk dripping steadily onto her hind legs, and a dejected look about her.

This, Alan knew, was a critical situation. Silk had no milk for the foal, and he needed that first drink – a special, rich milk called *colostrum* – within the first few

hours of his life, in order to get the antibodies and vita-
[illegible] his immune system and give him

[illegible]

carefully led the foal away [illegible]
stall, but Lisa would have nothing more to do with her infant son. If they could just hold Lisa still long enough for the colt to suck, she might change her mind, but the young mare was too confused and frightened, and her reactions grew increasingly violent with every attempt they made to bring him close to her. The foal began to tire and become upset, and Alan eventually had to return him to his "dry" mother. Time was running out for the baby. The longer he went without milk, the slimmer his chances of survival.

There was another option. Another of Alan's mares, a thoroughbred named Bonnie, had lost her foal just a couple of days before. She was an experienced brood-mare and still pining for her lost foal. There was a small chance that she might accept the colt. Alan hoped she wouldn't reject him, as raising an orphan foal is very hard work.

Lisa was milked and the colt was bottle-fed a first small meal of Lisa's colostrum before Bonnie was brought to the stable. It took very little persuasion for the older mare to accept Lisa's colt, and the confused baby, now onto his third mother, sucked greedily, fully filling his belly for the first time since his birth.

Within a few days, Bonnie and the colt had bonded well. The colt was independent right from the start, constantly worrying his foster dam with his wandering and exploring. Everyone agreed that he must be tough – he had survived his first challenge in life with flying colors.

He was a good-looking colt – a robust, straight-legged, dark bay with a small, white star on his broad forehead. He was a little small, but Alan wasn't worried about that. He had plenty of time to grow.

Alan decided to name him Kintamani Fosta because he was being fostered. Perhaps because of all the early human contact during his bonding hours, the bottle-feeding, or simply because he was born that way, Fosta had a sweet disposition and a natural liking of people. He was easy to halter train, friendly to deal with, and just a good-natured, curious boy right from the start. Alan, watching him develop and change every day, was impressed with the little colt. It was hard to say at that point what he might become, but if tenacity and spirit

...nything to do with it, he might just be a special

[illegible]

becom...

sport of endurance riding. He was a ta...

young man, and a horseman to the core. Endurance appealed to him – it challenged him physically and mentally, it was a friendly and social sport, and it upheld the highest ideals of horsemanship (animal welfare, viewing the horse as a partner rather than a commodity) more than any equine sport he had tried.

Alan's breeding program was aimed at producing horses for endurance, and was based around a talented young Arabian stallion named Arowana Mamaragan (God of Thunder in the Aboriginal language), or Ragan, for short. Alan had bought Ragan as a yearling, and he had proved to be as hardy and reliable as he was beautiful. Ragan was the base of many hopes and dreams, and he was the sire of the feisty bay colt.

Fosta spent the next few months at Bonnie's side, and in the companionship of another mare and her black colt, Dare. The colts were gelded while still with their dams and then weaned at about five months of age. Weaning is often a traumatic and unhappy time for young horses, but Fosta took it in stride, doing little more than whinnying for his dam a few times before turning his attention to the new pasture he was in. It was a new place to explore, and Mr. Independence wasn't about to waste time fretting when there were so many more interesting things to do. Besides, he still had Dare with him, and his people were hanging around more than they normally did, so what was there to worry about?

The two colts spent the following year and a half developing hard legs and lean muscles on the strong, natural pastures of Kintamani Stud. Fosta often led in breathtaking races and daring play fights, and he was always the first to the feed bucket. Dare was considerably larger than Fosta, but Fosta was proving to be the leader in every way.

The colts transformed from fuzzy weanlings, to lanky, ungainly yearlings, into elegant two year olds. They were strong, hard-muscled colts, with solid feet, pretty heads (the stamp of their sire), and healthy, shiny dark coats. Dare had grown tall and handsome and would soon start training. Fosta remained small, and Alan decided to give him an extra year to grow.

Fosta attended his first endurance ride that year, however. Alan was participating in the Wandandian ride with another horse, and the head vet, Dr. Roy Holland, asked him if he had any young horses he could bring to be used for demonstration purposes. Alan decided to bring Fosta.

Once again, Fosta's calm, gentle, people-loving nature served him well. Most colts, handled minimally for their first two years and pulled fresh from the pasture, would have found the trailer ride, the busy, unfamiliar camp life, and the vet demonstration unnerving, to say the least. Fosta was just fine. He was an easy demonstration subject of a horse too immature to race (endurance horses are not permitted to race until they are five years old), he adjusted easily to camp life, and he enjoyed the attention he received from the bored strappers who awaited the return of competing horses.

Alan, by then, was beginning to wonder if this first experience would be Fosta's only one. A horse of any size can be used for endurance, but Alan wasn't used to riding mere ponies, and he didn't plan to start now. A horse needed to be big enough to have a decent stride and carry a man over a hundred kilometers or more. Fosta wasn't looking very hopeful as a two year old.

By three, Fosta had reached a mere fourteen hands
high – too small, Alan thought, for a career in

3

The Walkers

Fosta soon found a new home with a young lady named Cathy Walker. Cathy and her mother, Susan, had spent several weeks looking for an experienced, older horse who could carry the teenager safely around the Pony Club courses and the streets and trails around Nowra, where they lived. A three-year-old, green-broke colt was definitely not what they had in mind.

The Walkers knew Alan Lindsay through other circles, and trusted him as an honest horseman when he told them he had a colt that might suit them. They

weren't having much luck finding their ideal horse, so
[illegible] look, but not to jump into any-

[illegible]

handled him all over. [illegible]
affectionate, and before they had spent an hour with him, they already knew that this would be their horse. Cathy summed him up when she said, "He's more person than he is horse."

Fosta moved to Nowra in June of 1984, and spent the following weeks getting to know his new people. The Walkers were completely taken with him and he quickly became a well-loved family member, rather than just a horse in the stable. Cathy rode him frequently, and soon trusted the young gelding completely, as he showed no signs of spookiness or misbehavior. His manners were impeccable, and it was easy to forget that he was still a very young and inexperienced riding horse. But he *was* still all of this, and forgetting that was a serious mistake.

Cathy became more emboldened as the days went on and was soon venturing out on the colt, following the back roads and trails of Nowra. Traffic was a new experience for Fosta, and, for the first time, he showed some nervousness, tensing and shying a little as cars went by, but never overreacting. The drivers were generally courteous, passing slowly, taking care not to frighten the horse and endanger the girl on his back. Had the exposure to traffic continued in this way, he would have become accustomed to it and it would have been excellent training for Fosta. But that was not to be.

On their way home from an outing one day, Cathy and Fosta were suddenly confronted by a large, speeding truck whose tarpaulin had worked loose and was flapping loudly.

Both of the youngsters panicked as the truck careened dangerously close to them. Fosta shied violently, and Cathy clutched at the colt with her legs and hands, trying to stop from being thrown. The sudden, strong pressure of her legs, which normally urged him forward, confused and frightened Fosta even more. To obey her would mean to move toward the terrifying truck. Fosta twisted farther from the road and started bucking – the first time he had ever attempted to buck a person from his back. Cathy soared over his head and landed hard in the ditch, where she could only watch helplessly, as the little bay bolted for home. The truck driver never bothered to stop.

Cathy, luckily, was shaken and a bit bruised, but otherwise unharmed. Fosta, however, was badly frightened by the incident, and from that day on, had a deeply ingrained fear of traffic that would plague him for the rest of his life.

Fosta's traffic phobia became a major problem for the Walkers. His immediate reaction to unexpected traffic was to buck and bolt. He was still wonderful in every other way, but this was a serious flaw – and a dangerous one. It was nearly impossible to avoid traffic altogether.

They tried everything they could think of to desensitize him, exposing him to "safe" traffic in calm ways as much as possible. He became tolerant of cars that he could see coming, but if they came along suddenly, or if he saw a truck of any kind, his reaction remained strong and decisive: buck and bolt.

Cathy tried to show him. She entered him in a halter class at a small, local event. The judge was very impressed with him. He was a handsome colt, moved nicely, and had lovely manners in hand. Everything was looking good as the judge stood at the center of the arena, ribbons in hand, ready to announce the winners of the class.

…mbled by. Fosta came unglued, spin-
…of control. He

the judge was no…
was not a safe road hack anymore, and…
a show horse, either.

The Walkers decided to look for a new horse for Cathy. She lacked the experience to deal with his problem, and they didn't want to risk her being hurt or losing her confidence. But Fosta had become such a loved part of the family that they were not ready to let him go.

Not wanting to have the young horse grow stagnant in a field, Cathy's mother, Susan, took up riding at the age of thirty-six. As a school horse, Fosta was lovely, patient, and gentle, and Susan enjoyed the hours she spent learning on him and trekking with her daughter on trails far from traffic. But, within a year of beginning, Susan discovered that she was pregnant with her fifth child. She couldn't risk a fall, and her riding days ended as suddenly as they had begun.

A close friend and horsewoman, Nina Klesnik, had met Fosta several times and knew his story from the Walkers. She was also familiar with Kintamani Stud and the endurance horses they bred. Nina was interested.

"I always thought I'd like to try endurance," she announced during one visit. "I wonder why the Lindsays didn't use Fosta for it."

"They thought he was too small," informed Susan. "But, he has grown a bit since we bought him. He's around fourteen and a half hands now – still small, but not too bad."

Nina didn't own a horse of her own at the time, and offered to ride him for the Walkers. She quickly grew attached to the affectionate little gelding. He was willing to do whatever she put him to, and did it with a friendly, happy spirit that made him a real joy to ride.

More and more, her mind went to the sport she knew Fosta had been bred for. She began to read about it, learning what she could through the pages of articles and books. The more she learned, the more she longed to try her hand at the challenge. She had the horse. She needed the opportunity – and a little help.

After getting the go-ahead from the Walkers, who were delighted to see Fosta being used, Nina turned to the person who knew the horse best. Alan Lindsay was

happy to give his advice, and curious to see Fosta. He
him to ever make it back into

heart, and lungs
work, climbing hills, crossing streams and rivers, follow-ing bush trails, ditches, and roadways. Fosta dumped her several times as they encountered the monster traffic, and she soon learned to never let go of the reins unless she wanted to be left on a trail with no horse to get her home.

By April, 1986, Nina decided she was ready to try her first test. She took Fosta to the Saddleback Mountain ride on the South Coast. They were not successful. Endurance is a very controlled sport, with stringent vet-erinary checkpoints along the courses to prevent the use of injured or exhausted animals. Nina, in her inexperi-ence, pushed Fosta too hard in the early going and he was pulled from the ride at the first vetting station when his pulse rate stayed too high for too long. He wasn't recovering from the stress quickly enough – a sign that he needed to stop.

Alan was also competing that day and was impressed with the little horse's poise and athleticism, even under stress. Something of the tenacity of that newborn colt was shining through, and he was curious to see where it would lead.

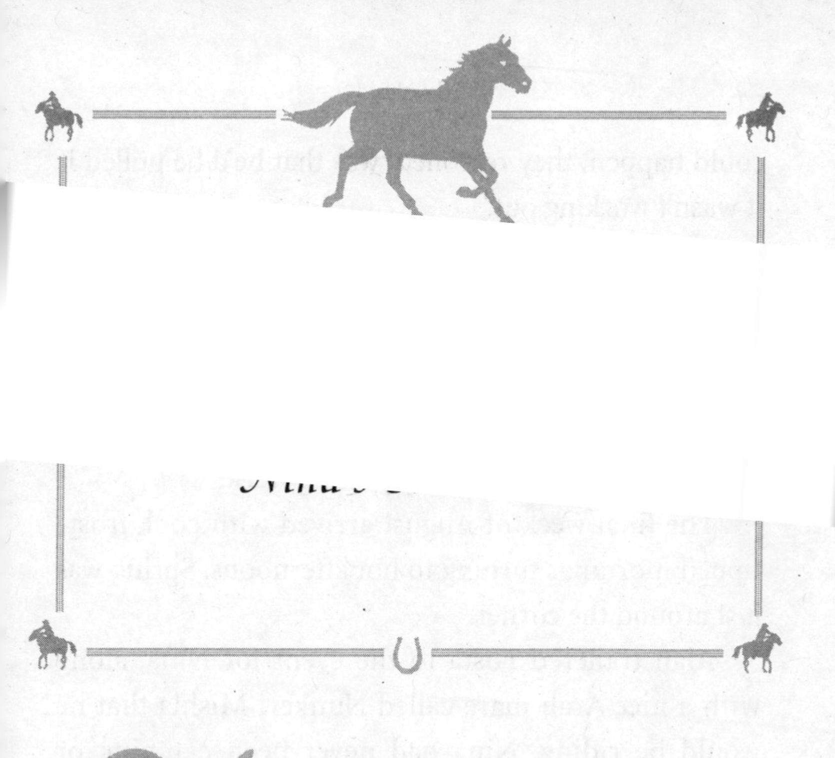

Nina decided that it would lead straight to Shahzada. It was the ultimate endurance challenge and something about it called to her.

When Nina announced to the Walkers that she intended to ride Fosta in the Shahzada that August, they were stunned. With only one attempt under his belt, and a non-completion at that, how did she possibly hope to compete in a four-hundred-kilometer ride? With some trepidation, they agreed to let her try. The worst that could happen, they reasoned, was that he'd be pulled if it wasn't working out.

With that trip to St. Albans in her sights, she rode whenever she could. Nina entered, and completed, a couple of short training rides with Fosta in Nowra and Jamberoo. Alan continued to work with her occasionally, and Fosta responded beautifully, becoming fitter and more mature with every passing week.

The final week of August arrived with cool, frost-tipped mornings turning to hot afternoons. Spring was just around the corner.

Alan trailered Fosta to the event for Nina, along with a nice Arab mare called Nunkeri Mishla that he would be riding. Nina had never been camping or ridden a test over several days, and Alan had advised her about what she would need to bring in order to survive the experience comfortably.

Unfortunately, something in his words must have been lost to her, because she arrived that day with a tent, but no tent poles, and only some rope and a few metal posts to set up a small yard for Fosta. She was flustered, but undaunted, and with a bit of help from the other competitors, soon had a shelter of sorts set up for herself between some trees, and a yard set up for Fosta, utilizing still more trees, her rope, and a few more borrowed

poles. It wasn't pretty, but by the time she was finished,
[illegible] and ready to face

[illegible]

need to gain experience [illegible]
completing this test, but newcomers to the sport were always welcomed and encouraged. Nina was soon drawn into the social spirit of the event and felt accepted and comfortable.

Fosta passed his pre-ride vet exam that Sunday afternoon, and in the evening, Nina joined the other riders for pre-ride instructions and maps. As she studied the complicated trails marked out on the papers, she began to feel the first twinges of doubt. She would have a hard time settling that night, although she knew that she and Fosta would need their rest if they were to have any chance of making it through this week.

The 3:00 a.m. call came all too soon. Bleary-eyed, Nina dressed in light layers and prepared for the early start. The air was chilly and she shivered as she double-checked her saddlebag to be sure she had packed everything she would need for the day's ride: a sponge, two syringes, electrolyte mix, a small first-aid kit, a hoof pick, a rubber emergency shoe, light snacks, sunscreen, a rain poncho, a water bottle, and tissues. She groomed Fosta carefully while he ate a light meal of grain and hay, checking every inch of him in the dark to make sure he hadn't injured himself in some way through the night.

She double-checked her tack, which she had cleaned scrupulously the evening before, and the tub full of equipment and feed that she would leave at the vetting station.

Finally, she saddled and bridled Fosta, and after about fifteen minutes of walking and trotting to warm him up, she joined the gathering crowd at the starting point. This would be the only shotgun start of the week. For the rest of the week, riders could choose their own starting times, as long as they completed the eighty kilometers they faced each day within twelve hours. Any rider still on course after 5:00 p.m. would be eliminated.

For the first time since arriving, Nina felt truly nervous. They'd had a bit of a rough start, and now four hundred kilometers lay before them. Challenging. Almost threatening. Had she made a mistake coming here? Were she and Fosta really ready for this?

Several other riders wished her luck as they rode past to take their place in the throng, but Nina could see in their eyes and the knowing smiles they gave

that her chances of

not

day. Exactly one hundred horses

morning when the pistol cracked at 4:00 a.m., some at a hard trot, others choosing to walk the first couple of kilometers. Within fifteen minutes, the starting area was empty and the race was under way.

Fosta was excited by the other horses and eager to keep up. It took a few kilometers before Nina could get him to settle into a relaxed pace, knowing that he would need to keep a lot in reserve if they were going to make it through the next five days. He had never completed more than forty kilometers before now. And neither had she.

The horse and rider teams negotiate the Shahzada trails in two legs – the morning leg being generally longer and tougher than the afternoon leg – with a compulsory one-hour rest stop in between. Each leg of the test consists of roadwork out of St. Albans (this proved to be the trickiest part for Fosta and Nina because of the potential for traffic encounters), a steep climb out of the valley, some distance across the high, rugged, countryside, a descent back into the valley, and roadwork back to the base camp and vetting area, utilizing different combinations of trails.

Monday morning wasn't so bad. Nina and Fosta were fresh and eager, and the fifty-two kilometers of trails that brought them three hundred meters above the valley floor were wonderful.

Back at base camp for the first break, Fosta passed his vet exam perfectly. His heart rate was surprisingly low and he had no lameness, good gut sounds, was well hydrated, and had not a mark on him. He was nearly as fresh starting the second leg as he had been in the morning.

He and Nina tackled the thirty-five kilometer afternoon leg gamely, climbing steeply up McKechnie's rocky track and descending just as steeply fifteen kilometers later. They were both tired when they returned to camp for the second time, but, again, Fosta passed the vet exam in great form. They had survived the first day.

At a community supper that evening, another rider congratulated Nina on her first day, but then said, teasingly, "Tomorrow is the day we separate the wheat from the chaff." Nina was too elated with her success of the first day and too tired to worry. Tomorrow would come enough. She'd deal with it then.

They climbed

goat path, in the chilly pre-dawn, feeling their way along by instinct as much as by eyesight. The cross-country section was winding and beautiful, but made them work, and the descent took them back along the rocky McKechnie trail. They were tired. Base camp was looking good. But, the leg wasn't over. Instead of heading right back to base, the ride map indicated a left turn, along Branch Road, across Clarie's Bridge, and to Preston's.

Preston's was the test! Nothing more than a rugged goat trail, having large sections where the climb angle was forty-five degrees, achieving a three-hundred-meter elevation climb and descent in about four kilometers of travel. It was exhausting and both Nina and Fosta struggled with the effort it required.

After that, the twenty kilometers back to St. Albans along the Wollombi Road was no problem. Fosta paid no attention to traffic or anything else. He was as eager as Nina to get back to base camp for a rest.

Fosta passed the vet exam, again with nice, low heart rates and a quick recovery from the stress of the morning. He was one of the lucky ones. When the afternoon leg started, there was a notable drop in the number of horses on the trail.

That leg, although shorter and easier, took them longer. Nina didn't push too hard, keeping Fosta at a slow and steady trot with very little fast work. Her own legs were feeling rather numb by then, from the hours in the saddle and the climbs of the past two days. Like most endurance riders, Nina chose to save her horse's back on the steepest climbs and "tail" up – letting the horse lead the way, while she followed behind on foot, holding his tail for support. Even with him pulling her up, the unaccustomed effort had been hard for her, and she rode that afternoon with an uncomfortable awareness of every muscle in her body. She wondered if Fosta was feeling the same way. He didn't complain. He never hesitated in his work, and moved along as though he were on a Sunday trail ride. It turned out that Fosta was wheat!

Tuesday night was the quietest night of the week. People were either too exhausted from the day's ride, or

too dejected about being vetted out to want to socialize very heartily. Three more days lay ahead, and at that point, those three days – those two hundred forty remaining kilometers – seemed like an eternity.

Nina had a tough time crawling out of her sleeping bag Wednesday morning. Her muscles were stiff, her whole being just wanted to sleep and sleep. But as she lay there, thinking about the past two days, and of the day ahead of them, she began to feel excited. She had never pushed herself like this before, and she was making it. She had learned so much in the past two days, and she and Fosta had come so far as a team. She ignored the aches and pains, slipped out of her funny little tent, and went quietly to where Fosta stood, dozing.

He lifted his head at her approach and nickered softly. She stood with him there in the darkness, stroking him, telling him how proud she was of him, and feeling more deeply connected to him than she had ever felt to any other animal.

Nina thoroughly enjoyed the ride on Wednesday. She and Fosta seemed to have found their stride. The trails were slightly easier, although still very challenging, and the views along the way were breathtaking. They made good time, passed every vet inspection with flying and finished the day fresher than they had any

Fosta was also feeling good. He had been quiet the first few nights in his little makeshift yard, content to eat and rest. But by Wednesday night, he had eaten down most of the grass in his enclosure and he was beginning to feel restless. He cleaned up the hay Nina had left him for the night, but the grass outside his rope fence beckoned to him. It didn't take him long to figure out how to escape the simple enclosure, and he spent the rest of the night wandering the banks of the shallow McDonald River, enjoying a hearty meal of greens and a wonderful, midnight freedom.

When Nina woke Thursday morning and found him gone, she was frantic. News of the missing horse spread quickly to the other teams, and everyone kept an eye out for the little bay gelding.

Eventually he was found. Someone had spotted him earlier that morning, and had caught him and tied him in their yard before starting their ride for the day. Nina had decided to leave slightly later that morning, and was now facing quite a late start.

Fosta seemed unharmed by his night's excursion, so she prepared him as usual and hoped that he had not used up too much of the energy he would need to get through that day. They would have to make up a bit of time in order to finish by the 5:00 p.m. deadline.

They had gone less than a third of the way around the first leg when Nina knew something was wrong. Fosta was not striding out as strongly as usual, and seemed to be struggling a bit on the first climbs. By the time they leveled out on the Great Northern Road, he was definitely favoring a leg, and she knew they'd have to stop.

Nina was disappointed, but only slightly. They had gone a long way for their first try, and she was proud of herself, and of Fosta. The experience had changed Nina, given her confidence in her own abilities, and sparked a passion in her for endurance that would carry her forward into the challenges ahead.

She returned Fosta to the Walkers, having made up her mind to start looking for a horse of her own. Like most endurance riders, she had her sights set on a pure-bred Arabian, the breed that excels at endurance above all others. Fosta had paved the way. Now it was time to [illegible]

[illegible]

his way ever [illegible]

The Walkers were now back in the position of wondering what to do with him, but for now, it didn't matter. They'd give it some time and decide later. They were not interested in endurance, and it looked as though his first season – a season of incompletions – just might be his last.

5
A Second Chance

Fosta would get a chance to race again. A wealthy couple from the northern suburbs of Sydney had seen his potential at Shahzada and phoned Susan with an offer to buy him. At first, Susan declined the offer, but after Adele Hayles continued to phone her, once a week for six weeks, the Walkers decided it was time to let him go.

Fosta seemed to understand, somehow, what had happened. The little horse that had never shown anything but gentle affection toward the Walkers the whole time they had owned him, bit Susan on the thigh – hard!

Saying good-bye to him was harder than any of them had

... Susan made Adele promise

...

manners were so impeccable ...

Adele hadn't worried about it. She had been sure that in the right hands, it was a problem they could overcome.

Adele entered Fosta in only one test, the eighty-kilometer Bullio ride in May, 1987. They completed the ride successfully, but Adele was not impressed by his times.

Fosta also appeared on "Simon Townsend's Wonder World," a popular children's television series, demonstrating the sport of endurance. But he and Adele never found their stride together, and about fifteen months after she had bought him, after being bucked off one too many times, Adele phoned the Walkers to see if they wanted him back.

The Walkers were in a quandary, then. They had just bought Cathy a second horse and were not in a position to buy Fosta back. They remained deeply attached to him, however, and were reluctant to see him sold to yet another home, especially since his dangerous fault seemed to be limiting his uses and his chances at staying with an owner for any length of time.

Susan decided to contact Alan Lindsay and let him know the situation. It was a good move. Alan was intrigued by the prospect of having Fosta back. The little bay had shown something at Shahzada that he had liked, and although it had taken an unusually long time, Fosta had finally matured to a somewhat better size, standing now at his full, mature height of fifteen hands. He wasn't a big horse, but at least he wasn't a pony anymore. Alan decided to give him a try.

Throughout that spring, Alan worked with Fosta, training him and getting to know him well. Fosta was an enthusiastic partner and gave his all, seeming to enjoy every minute he spent with his first owner. His affectionate nickers and patient manners during the hours they spent together on the trails soon made him as well loved by Alan and Helen Lindsay as he had been by the Walkers.

Four or five days a week they would head out, walking the first kilometer or so, then trotting and cantering for up to ten kilometers. On the way home, some fast hill work, and then a cooling walk the rest of the way back. After his workout, Fosta enjoyed a hose-down, and his favorite part of the day, the sand roll, where all

his muscles

come to be known in the Lindsay household, passed

test impressively. Alan decided to enter him as his mount for the August Shahzada.

Alan and a close friend and fellow endurance competitor, John Robertson, entered the Shac, a twenty-kilometer *ride and tie* event that summer, just for fun.

The ride and tie involves two people and one horse. One person rides a while, then ties the horse up, and starts to run, while the second person runs, catches up to where the horse is tied, gets on, and rides for a while, before tying the horse and running again. A crazy relay race of sorts, and just the right game for a level-headed horse and a couple of athletic, competitive, fit, young men. Alan had chosen Fosta as their horse, and he was the perfect partner, waiting calmly on his own until John or Alan arrived, then kicking into gear and going hard for a few kilometers, then calming right back down when it was time to wait again.

John had met Fosta before then, but had never had the opportunity to ride him. He thoroughly enjoyed the horse that day, and, on a bit of a whim, made an offer to buy him. Alan accepted the offer, with the agreement that he still get to ride Fosta in the upcoming Shahzada.

"I just have a feeling about him," Alan explained when John questioned his request. "He's been tough from the start, and slow to mature. I don't think we've seen the best of him yet. I'd really like the chance to test him and see what he's made of. Besides, if he does well, it looks good on Ragan's record, too."

He was tested only lightly that year, but gained strength in every ride, finishing seventh in the hundred-kilometer Shoalhaven ride for the Robertsons in July. From there, all focus was turned to the final week of August. When the time finally arrived, Fosta and Alan were ready.

The 1987 Shahzada was a far different experience for Fosta than his trip with Nina had been the year before. There would be no midnight escapades along the banks of the river this time, or strange rustlings from a makeshift tent. The Lindsays camped in a comfortable trailer close to the securely constructed, small yard that was Foz's temporary home. He ate warm, molasses bran mashes and rested with Epsom salts bandages soothing

his tired legs. Massages and frequent walks throughout the evenings reduced the stiffening of his muscles, and a daily roll on the sandy riverbank worked out the final itches. Nothing about his care or comfort was overlooked, and he earned every bit of it.

Fosta wasn't held at the back of the pack during the Monday morning shotgun start this year, but quickly found his place near the front-runners, and settled into the good, strong working trot that Alan knew he could maintain for mile after mile.

Unlike the thoroughbred racehorses, bred to gallop at tremendous speeds for short amounts of time, the endurance horse is bred and trained to trot. The trot is the most efficient of the equine gaits and a fit, sound horse can maintain a steady trot for a very long time without undue stress. The trick is in knowing how hard to push before it becomes stressful, how long to ask the horse to keep it up, and how much weight he can carry before it affects his ability to work at his best. Alan could read a horse well, and he had come to know Fosta inside and out over the past months. They settled into their pace, confidently facing the four hundred kilometers before them.

Alan was a good rider and a competitive man, and he brought out the best in Foz. He spent as much time off the horse's back – tailing up the daunting hills and running down the other side, and jogging beside his

vetting station, and, going into the final day,

place for a top-ten finish.

Ninety-six horses had taken the test. More than thirty of those had already failed. The leading riders were setting an extraordinarily fast pace, completing the daily eighty kilometers in approximately five and a half to six hours each day. Fosta and Alan were only a fraction slower than the front-runners all week.

Alan was in high spirits when they hit the trail Friday morning. Fosta seemed to feel his mood and moved out as eagerly as if they were just beginning the four-hundred-kilometer trek. They made easy work of the long, hard morning leg, vetted perfectly, and attacked the final thirty kilometers in the afternoon with gusto. They were fourth when they entered base camp for the final time, with an excellent time of 30.56 hours. When they were selected for the Best Conditioned Horse parade and judging, Alan was doubly pleased.

The Best Conditioned judging would take place during the awards ceremony the next morning. Every rider who finishes the ride within the time limits and with a healthy horse earns a buckle. Ten horses are selected to parade and are judged for the coveted Best Conditioned Horse award, considered the highest accolade in the sport. Each of these ten horses earns a sash, and the horse deemed most able to continue racing is awarded a pewter plate. There is no prize for the fastest time, although many serious competitors compete to break this record. Finishing in a top-ten position is an honor, although finishing at all is considered a win. There are no cash prizes and no organized betting. Riders who choose to try their hand at Shahzada do so for the challenge, and a pure love of horses. Alan Lindsay exemplified the ideals of an endurance rider and he earned his rewards honestly.

Saturday morning, Alan earned his completion buckle and Fosta wore the sash for being one of the ten best-managed horses. Foz was glowing with good health and looking every bit ready to continue for another day. Alan was all smiles as he accepted the Best Conditioned pewter plate. Best of all, the game little gelding earned more hugs and treats then he knew what to do with, and a very well-deserved rest.

John Robertson was delighted with his new horse,

Within six

farm, Fosta's new family split up, and, once again, his future was up in the air. It was a troublesome, messy breakdown, and when the dust cleared, Fosta belonged to John's wife as part of her separation deal. Foz would stay with John until she settled into a new home, but then he'd have to leave Cambewarra again.

In the months following this sad affair, John threw himself into the horses and competition as he never had before. He had demons to outrun, and in the challenge of the rides, he found a pleasure and a sense of success that was eluding him in other areas of his life at that time. Fosta, fresh off his outstanding achievement at Shahzada, in his prime, sound and fit, was the perfect partner for a driven young man, and together, they found success on the marathon trails in 1988.

They conquered the eighty-kilometer Pigeon House Mountain ride in March, finishing a close second and winning the Best Conditioned award. They ran second again in April in the eighty-kilometer Saddleback Mountain ride, but were vetted out due to an eye injury Fosta received in the final kilometers. In May, recovered and fresh, they ran yet another second in the eighty-kilometer Tantawanglo ride. Little Foz was looking better all the time, and John hoped he'd still be around for Shahzada.

He was, and on the last week of August, he again made the journey to St. Albans to face the four-hundred-kilometer test, this time with rider number three. John knew that completing the test once was a major accomplishment for any horse, but he felt certain that Foz had another strong shot at doing it again. Fosta had the perfect combination of youth, experience, manners, and toughness. Traffic still troubled him – John had sat in the dust many a time, watching the panicked gelding running for home. There seemed to be no real rhyme or reason to his fears anymore. He'd be fine for the longest time, then a certain vehicle would drive by, and he'd completely fall apart. Otherwise, he was game, cooperative, and always an affectionate, gentle companion.

The weather proved to be a factor this time around, with colder mornings, wetter trails, and occasional hot spells in the afternoons. John rode the Shahzada carefully, sticking near the leaders, but never pushing Fosta

[illegible] steep, rocky climbs

[illegible]

been the past two years.

Despite the more difficult conditions, Saturday morning found Fosta being awarded for a top-ten completion once again. He had finished a slow but solid seventh, injury free, but tired. John was very pleased with him, and so was Alan Lindsay, who was beginning to think more highly of the little horse all the time. Two top-ten completions in the longest, toughest ride in Australia. It was something to be proud of.

Unfortunately, it would be the last time Fosta would race for quite a while.

Within a few months of his Shahzada test, Fosta found himself heading for the Snowy Mountains, and a new home near Berridale, where he would reside, largely unused, for the next year. John's wife had also been involved in the sport of endurance, and she knew she had a great little horse in her stable yard, but she wasn't in a situation to do much about it at the time.

Eventually, life began to sort itself out for Fosta's owner, and she realized that she would not be the best person to own the spunky gelding. He deserved better. She did not offer him back to John, but called Alan Lindsay, who had moved his family and farm to Cowra the year before. Once again, Fosta would return to Kintamani. This time he would stay.

Big Dreams

Alan and Helen worked with the gelding in the coming months, rebuilding his base fitness level and getting him back into racing form. Foz seemed happy to be home and happy to be working again, giving his all to these people he knew and loved more than anyone.

Alan had his sights set on Shahzada again, but there wasn't a lot of time to prepare and he knew it would be tough after more than a year off. He and Fosta completed the eighty-kilometer Wandandian ride, which helped put some of the edge back on the little horse, but it was hard to say if he was ready to pull off another four-hundred-kilometer test. It was hard to say if any horse was ever ready for such a test!

One hundred twenty-three horses were entered for the Shahzada that August – one of the largest fields ever. The weather was not a factor that year. The skies were clear, the afternoons warm and dry, and the river full of water. It was the trails that caused the greatest problems for the teams. Many new routes had been marked, the hills were treacherous, and some of the old routes that were still being used were worn, rocky, and full of new-growth brush. The horses felt the stress and had a difficult time with the challenging course. Only half would complete the test, including Fosta.

Fosta had an uncanny ability for covering the courses cleanly, making his way through rock and bush without picking up a scratch. He was sure-footed and calm, and seemed to know, instinctively, the best routes to take. Alan was happy to let Foz make decisions, and trusted the horse to get them through the sticky spots in one piece. Fosta never failed.

Alan helped him all he could, jogging countless kilometers beside the bay, keeping him nourished, cool, and limber during the rest periods, and trying to prevent his own discomfort from affecting his partner's

They were an awesome team, a combina-

from racing, the

handful of horses achieved multiple completions in this grueling test – they were the second to cross the finish line. Unfortunately, the final stretch of the test had taken its toll on the first-place finisher and he did not pass the vet inspection. Alan and Fosta were boosted to the number one position.

No one had expected him to be in the top ten that year. Certainly, no one expected him to be first.

Kintamani Fosta turned eleven in 1991, and was now an experienced long distance horse, and a seasoned competitor. His fear of traffic remained his greatest downfall, despite the Lindsays' continued efforts to condition him to accept it. Most endurance rides involve highway crossings and exposure to vehicles, and every outing was a gamble with Fosta. Most of the time he was fine, but now and then, all hell would break loose. The Lindsays were bucked off a lot less than most of his previous riders had been, however, and they soon learned to accommodate his phobia, keeping him far from the edge of the road, if they had to travel roadways at all, and being well prepared for his antics.

In every other way, Foz remained one of the sweetest natured horses the Lindsays had ever bred and raised. He was an unusually expressive horse and his likes and dislikes came through loud and clear!

He loved anything sweet – cakes, breads, carrots, and a special molasses water that Helen prepared for him. He loved the company of people, especially children, and showed the most incredible patience and gentleness toward Helen and Alan's young son, Mark.

He did not like being left alone, or being late for meals, and each crime was considered a good excuse for bashing whatever was handy (a gate, bucket, fence rail) with his front hooves. The racket soon brought someone running to prevent him from injuring himself, and so it was quite effective.

Fosta was a master of gate latches, and frequently went on afternoon escapades around the farm. The young gentleman, normally so cooperative and easy to catch, was suddenly impossible, and would spend hours evading his frustrated owners as he darted behind sheds, trees, and horse yards, stopping only long enough to tease the mares (he loved to show off for the mares), bite of grass along the way. It was cheeky fun,

he and Helen had moved the Kintamani sign
to a larger, four-hundred-acre farm, still in the Cowra area, and they were preparing for the birth of their second child. They had several horses in competition, plus the breeding horses to deal with, and Foz ended up having a pretty easy year of it.

St. Albans was in the plans again, however. They might miss every other test that year, but they wouldn't miss Shahzada. It would be Fosta's fifth attempt, and it was starting to look like *his* race. Something in Alan was challenged to try again, to see how far the little horse could go.

With only a couple of short weeks to go before the marathon, Alan entered Foz in the eighty-kilometer Nowra ride. Fosta managed it successfully, and it accomplished what Alan had hoped for, putting a mental sharpness and an edge of fitness on Fosta that only a real race could accomplish.

Fosta and Alan joined one hundred fourteen horse-and-rider teams at the start of Shahzada that year. The weather was excellent, the trails clear and dry, and the leaders had soon set a blistering pace, only a fraction slower than the 1986 record time. Fosta and Alan were one of the front-runners, and Alan wondered if they could repeat their first-place finish of the year before. Fosta seemed better than he ever had. He loved the job he had been bred for and grew more enthusiastic with every passing kilometer. His stamina seemed to have no limits, and Alan pushed him just a little harder, confident they could hold up for the five days.

They did hold up, and held up well, but the leaders were eating up the trail at a grueling pace, and by the third day, Alan knew that if he rode in search of a first-place finish, he would have to push too hard and take risks he wasn't prepared to take with his game mount. He aimed, instead, for a sound top ten, and they ended up fourth of the sixty-three horses that completed the ride. Fosta had completed the test in his best time ever, covering the four hundred kilometers in 28.08 hours. That was three hours faster than his winning time of the year before, and yet another accomplishment to be proud of.

Alan and Helen were excited and looking forward

to the coming race season. Alan couldn't help but brag

and one first! He's so much better than

he'd be, and I don't think he's done yet."

The Lindsays entered Fosta in the hundred-kilometer East Kurrajong ride just a couple of weeks later, and Foz performed excellently again, completing the one-day test in third place, again in fast time. It seemed that Fosta had come into his own and was ready to show the world what he was made of.

In November, Alan and Helen were blessed with the birth of a beautiful baby girl, whom they named Erica. It was the icing on the cake of a life that was happy and full for the couple. Their farm was a success, Alan had won the National Distance Rider of the Year Award, he had a good job, a lovely, growing family, and an abundance of solid friendships.

But, there would be challenges that year. Shortly after Erica's arrival, a filly was bitten by a brown snake while grazing in her pasture. Venomous snakes are not uncommon in New South Wales, and many a curious horse investigating a movement in the grass has found itself bitten on the face or neck, soon struggling to breath as its airways begin to swell shut. Only a few horses actually die from snakebites each year, but a bite from a brown snake can be fatal if undiscovered and untreated. The Lindsays found the filly too late, and she died an agonizing death of paralysis, internal bleeding, and suffocation.

One week later, a second horse was bitten – a small bay gelding with a heart as big as a house. Helen's father found him standing over his water, unable to bend his neck, and looking decidedly in distress. The puncture wounds from the snake's fangs were found on his neck.

A vet was summoned quickly and was soon pumping massive doses of antivenin and fluids into Fosta's veins. It was touch and go for a while, but the spirit of the orphaned foal shone through, and Fosta survived that day. He was not well though, and his struggle was far from over.

The snakebite had taken a terrible toll on Fosta's body, and he was unable to eat or move. He seemed unable to shake the pain and paralysis and over the following weeks, the Lindsays could only watch in despair

as their beautiful friend dwindled away to a mere shadow of the fit and healthy horse he had been. Within three weeks, despite the best of care, he was a wrack of bones, and still refusing to eat or walk at all. He was desperately ill and soon reached a critical state. The vet advised that if no improvement were seen in the next couple of days, they would have to start intravenous nourishment to keep him alive.

Perhaps it was mere coincidence, or maybe Fosta had understood the vet's words somehow, but the next day, he started to move – one slow, painful step, then another and another, stopping to rest with each attempt. He began to nibble at the tips of the grass in his paddock and accept small handfuls of warm, sweet, bran mash, although he still refused his hay and grain. Over the days and weeks that followed, he began to improve, slowly but definitely, and the Lindsays were extremely relieved. They had come to really love the personable little horse, and losing him would have been a real blow to their family.

Within a few more weeks, Foz had regained his usual healthy appetite, and by the New Year, had recovered most of his lost body weight. The Lindsays were well aware that bites from a brown snake often result in career-ending kidney and liver damage, and they were prepared for the worst when the vet ran a series of

[illegible] Remarkably, there

[illegible]

watching carefully all the time for signs of [illegible]

Fosta improved with every outing, regaining his muscle strength and his spirit. By April, Alan decided he was ready to try again.

They entered Fosta in the one-hundred-kilometer Gundagai ride near the end of April, and let him run the test at his own speed. Fosta completed the test in the slow time of just over nine hours, but he was gleaming with health at the end. Alan was pleased. "I think you're ready to go again, aren't you Fozzy?" Fosta tossed his head as though he understood and shared Alan's eagerness for the coming challenges.

7

Marathon Master

Two weeks later, Fosta cleared away any doubts that may have lingered about his recovery and ability to compete, when he ran a fast second in the one-hundred-kilometer Wagga ride.

He competed steadily for the rest of that season, racking up another three hundred twenty kilometers and an important Tom Quilty buckle (another of the longer, more prestigious endurance rides in Australia), before heading, once again, to St. Albans in August.

Helen rode Fosta as often as Alan that year, and it

would be her turn to try her hand at Shahzada. The

dawdle on the trail, knowing that the infant would be growing hungry and impatient by the end of each leg. Fosta made easy work of the challenging course, and the pair finished the week in the top five once more. Fosta had accomplished the feat that forty-one horses out of the ninety-nine who started could not accomplish, and had made it look easy. He just seemed to get better and better. Many people were beginning to wonder how many times he could conquer this test before *it* defeated *him*.

"I'm just glad he kept coming back home to us," said a tired Helen that Friday night. "All the bucking and shying in the world wouldn't make us want to sell him now."

The Lindsays gave Fosta the rest of that year off, but he was back under saddle again early in the New Year. They campaigned hard in 1993, racking up over thirteen hundred kilometers in nine successfully completed rides. Foz finished in the top ten in every one of the tests.

When it was time to travel to St. Albans that year, Fosta was as ready as he'd ever been. He was hard, fit, solid muscle, and both mentally and physically sound. Helen had been riding him most of that year, and she was confident that Fosta would be able to earn his sixth buckle at this test.

But on Sunday, as they set up camp and prepared for the first of the vet inspections, Helen was feeling under the weather. She tried to ignore it all afternoon, but by evening, she could no longer deny the nausea, fever, and weakness of a sudden flu, and she knew she would not be able to ride in the morning.

A close friend, Louise McCormack, was having difficulties of her own that day. It was her first attempt at Shahzada, and she was eager to test a nice mare she had brought along. Unfortunately, within hours of setting up, the mare had injured her shoulder while rolling in her makeshift yard, and had come up quite lame. Louise knew she would not pass the vet inspection, and voluntarily withdrew her horse.

The solution was obvious. Fosta was needing a rider, and Louise was needing a horse, and since they were there for the week anyway (Alan was riding another of their

horses in the test), Helen decided to offer Fosta to Louise.
hours to get to

complete the test again, but with an [illegible]
marathoner on his back, the chances were much slimmer, and another top ten completion was almost out of the question.

However, Fosta was quick to adjust to his new rider's weight and style of riding, and soon found that she was giving him a lot of the controls. Louise was well aware that he knew these difficult trails far better than she did, and she gave him rein to make the decisions.

With the help of the Lindsays at the vet stops, her own sheer determination, and the easy way Fosta managed the kilometers and obstacles that stopped forty-one percent of the ninety-three horses entered that year, the pair did what no one expected them to do. They finished with a slow time of 38:09 hours, but they were ninth. Once again, Fosta had made the top ten and completed the grueling test like a pro, this time with his fourth rider. He was in remarkable form, and ready for the best year of his life.

There was no rest for Fosta at the end of 1993, with his last test the one-hundred-twenty-kilometer Adaminaby in December, and his first ride of 1994, the eighty-kilometer Whitton, in January.

At fourteen years old, Kintamani Fosta was the picture of health – lean and muscular, with clean, sound limbs, a shining red coat, and hard hooves. He loved the rides and the time he spent with his people, and he took care of them on the trails just as much as they took care of him. The little bay gelding was reliable and kind, and was always willing to do just a little more.

Fosta took on the ultra-important task of teaching the Linsdays' seven-year-old son, Mark, to ride that year. With the patience of an old schoolmaster, the seasoned competitor carried the boy, helping him gain balance, skill, and, most importantly, confidence. Before long, they were entering short "trainers" (twenty- to forty-kilometer rides), and a new generation of endurance competitor was on its way.

It was little Mark who entered Fosta in the Whitton ride in December. It would be his first real endurance test, and he was proud and excited. There were several other youngsters at the ride, and Mark was eager to [illegible] all the cool things he could do. [illegible]

[illegible] came up, it struck Mark's forehead, and the [illegible] were soon on their way to the local hospital for stitches. Despite a late night and a quick recovery from a little shock, Mark decided he wanted to ride anyway.

Alan mounted Bindo, Fosta's best friend and another of the Lindsays' troopers, and rode out beside his son. By the first vet stop at forty kilometers, Mark was pale and unhappy, and obviously too tired to go on. Fosta was pulled from the ride, and Alan went on with Bindo to complete the final leg of the test alone. For Fosta, it would be the first of many rides with the precious cargo of the youngest Lindsay family members on his back, but his main rider that year would, again, be Helen.

Helen and Fosta entered, and successfully completed, fourteen rides in a row that year, covering one thousand, six hundred sixty kilometers of some of the most rugged trails in Australia. The gutsy little horse picked up his third Tom Quilty buckle, finished in the top ten in over half the rides, and had one of the best Shahzada tests of his career.

The weather for Shahzada was glorious that last week of winter, with cool mornings, but temperatures reaching the thirties by the afternoons. The trails were hard and dry, and the river water low. Ninety-eight teams entered that year, and a higher number than average, a full sixty percent, would complete the test. Leading the way was a small, tough, affectionate bay gelding named Kintamani Fosta.

Helen and Fosta had started the week off slowly, as Alan was riding his new stallion, Silver Shadow, for the first time around the test. The young stallion was nervous and unaccustomed to going around groups of horses on the trail, walking into dams full of horses and relaxing enough to drink, and negotiating the difficult inclines and descents that made the Shahzada test so challenging. "Uncle Foz" stayed beside him through those first days, paving the way and helping him gain much-needed confidence.

Silver Shadow and Fosta worked slowly and steadily through that Monday, and pulled through the "Widow Breaker" Tuesday in one piece. By Wednesday, the younger horse was well settled, focused only on the job at hand, too tired for any extra shenanigans. He and Foz

was trotting hard, leaving his young student behind.

Over the next two days, Fosta and Helen gained ground on the front teams, eventually taking the lead. Foz was in superb form, running on automatic, devouring the trail, kilometer after kilometer.

It was an elated Helen who rode Fosta into the vetting station for the final time that week, and her elation increased when she learned that he had been called up for the Best Conditioned parade. They had completed the test in 32.20 hours, traveling much faster over the last two and a half days than they had the first. It was Fosta's seventh Shahzada buckle in eight attempts, all for top ten placings, his second win, and his fourth time being paraded for Best Conditioned.

Fosta had now proven himself, beyond a doubt, to be a top-notch endurance horse. Few horses were competing with the drive and consistency of this little gelding, and he wasn't finished yet.

Three more successful rides followed Shahzada that year, setting Fosta in position to earn the well-deserved titles of National Distance Horse of the Year and NSW Distance Horse of the Year. It was a brilliant end to an outstanding year, and the Lindsays couldn't have been happier with him.

Helen Brown's Shahzada

Helen and Alan decided to give Fosta a well-earned break, while they concentrated on some of the upcoming competitors from their farm. For a few months, Foz and his best friend, Bindo, relaxed in the rolling hillside pastures of Kintamani Stud, watching lazily as mobs of kangaroo moved across the valley, dozing in the strong sunshine that baked the grasses and warmed their skin, and simply taking life easy. Minor injuries healed, tired muscles rejuvenated, and mental fatigue soon gave way to high spirits and playfulness. It wasn't long before Foz was bashing at the gate again, seeking attention from his people, eager to get back into action.

The Lindsays were campaigning with several other horses by then, but they put Fosta back into training, hoping to have him ready for a few rides toward the end of winter, including Shahzada, of course. The trouble was in deciding who would be able to ride him that year.

In the end, it was not Alan or Helen who rode him around the demanding course, but another Helen – a good friend of the Lindsays named Helen Brown. She had tried her hand at Shahzada only once before, but she had not been lucky, vetting out with a lame horse on the last day of the test. She had strapped for Helen Lindsay the year before, contributing greatly to their success, and she was an easy choice of rider for the Lindsays to consider. When Helen Lindsay offered her friend the chance to ride "Mr. Automatic" in the 1995 event, Helen Brown was delighted.

It was decided that Fosta and Helen Brown needed a pre-Shahzada ride, to get to know one another and give Foz the edge back that a few months at pasture had taken off.

They completed the eighty-kilometer Yengo ride in July in slow time, but the test served its purpose. Fosta

this year's Shahzada would be

blessings and curses

that assembled at the starting line

morning.

Helen Brown traveled to St. Albans with the Lindsays, and Fosta settled in for his ninth attempt at the daunting four hundred kilometers that lay before them. The extreme heat made the job of maintaining body fluids and electrolytes harder than normal, and the water that was available along the trail was warm and murky. The opportunities for cooling down and drinking were far fewer than normal. This would have a severe impact on the teams, and within the first few days, almost half of the horses had been pulled at the vetting stations. The conditions would take their toll on Fosta as well.

They made it through Monday in good form, traveling at a steady pace and keeping within an hour or so of the top ten runners.

Tuesday dawned hot and forbidding – the toughest day of the test lay directly ahead of them, and it was clear from the start, the heat would be the biggest factor to deal with that day. By noon, both horses and riders were sweating profusely, and the state of the water on the trail was a real concern. Fosta held up, but it took a lot out of him.

Conditions did not improve for the Wednesday stretch, and about halfway through the tough morning leg, Fosta and Helen began having problems. Fosta had been working hard and was thirsty when they came to a shallow, slow-running creek. The water had been stirred up by other horses that had passed by recently, and it was red, silty, and warm. Fosta drank deeply.

Within an hour, he was showing signs of discomfort, not wanting to stride out, resisting Helen's cues, and asking to stop. Helen let him graze a while, watching carefully as he kicked at his belly, moved around her restlessly, and complained about the tummy ache – colic – that was bothering him. Helen also noticed that his stools were small, hard balls instead of the usual big, soft lumps. These were all potentially serious signs, and it was uncertain whether Fosta would be able to continue.

Helen and Fosta moved slowly then, working their way toward the base camp and vetting station, and the one-hour rest period.

...eed that it looked like

...had water

his ...

quently, encourag...

They sponged his body to coo...

constantly.

They took him to a grassy area and allowed him free range of the greenery, knowing that it would be vital for him to eat if he were to have enough energy for the second leg of the day, and knowing, also, that green grass would add moisture and fiber to his intestines and would move through his system far more easily than dry hay.

By the end of the hour, Foz seemed to be more comfortable, responding in his usual affectionate way, and looking more relaxed. It seemed to be a mild bout of colic, but his people were concerned about putting him back out on the trail.

They waited a while longer, continuing to walk Fosta, offering him water and grass, and waiting for him to pass another stool. The attending veterinarian agreed that it seemed like a mild case and recommended that they keep going, but take it easy, and make sure he got plenty of water. His heart rate had dropped nicely, his gut sounds were normal, his capillary refill test indicated that he was well hydrated, there were no signs of lameness – Foz was cleared to go on.

Still, the Lindsays waited, until finally, he pooped. A nice, moist, squishy poop. It was the sign they had been waiting for. Within ten minutes, Fosta and Helen were back on the course, but they had lost a lot of time and were now well behind the front-runners.

Within five kilometers of starting the afternoon leg, Helen felt Fosta kick back into gear. He shied at a street sign, trotted out strongly, and seemed to have regained his usual spirit and courage.

Fosta and Helen were doing all right together, although this new rider liked to make the decisions more than he was used to, and had a few things to learn. They were on one of the toughest parts of the course when Fosta finally decided to tell her how it was.

They were traversing the "Steps," a steep, rocky, dangerous bit of trail, and Helen was off Fosta's back, tailing him. Ahead of them, the trail suddenly cut to the right, but Helen could see riders up ahead of them on the trail that went straight ahead, and so she urged Foz to go straight on. Fosta stopped, refusing to go forward, and

… the right. Helen

…rong

highly un…
to the Lindsays that sh…
at her!), and then stopped dead ag…
Helen realized her mistake. They were stuck on …
with several other horses, a steep drop directly in front
of them, and no way to turn around.

Foz refused to back up, or move in any direction. He
had tried to tell her the right way and she had refused to
listen, so now it was up to her to solve the problem
herself. Finally, frustrated and humiliated, Helen crawled
between his legs to his head and apologized. As though
he understood her perfectly, he began backing down the
trail with the calmness and manners of a true gentleman, and they were on their way once again – on the
trail heading to the right! From then on, Helen gave him
his head any time she was in doubt, and trusted him to
lead the way. And he did.

By the end of the week, they had gained back some
of the ground they had lost on the Wednesday, but not
enough for a top ten completion. They completed the
test in fine form, ranking twelfth in 42.30 hours, and

Best Conditioned. The

eighth

finally realized

9

Milestones

1996 would mark the first time in ten years that the name Kintamani Fosta was not on the list of horses at St. Albans in August. Other horses, younger horses, were taking the stage now, and the regulars at Shahzada assumed that Fosta would not compete there again. Eight completions out of nine attempts was an outstanding accomplishment, something the Lindsays could really be pleased about. Maybe it was time to call it quits.

But Fosta wasn't finished. He was a regular competitor that year, successfully completing six rides over four doing it in his usual style.

now nine

year, Fosta ca

eighty-kilometer rides, and o

at Binya, they earned the Junior Best Condi

Fosta was still a tough little horse to beat.

Fosta turned seventeen in 1997. His coat still glowed a deep, shining red-bay, accentuated by the wispy, flowing black mane and tail, and the neat white star on his forehead. He was the picture of middle-aged health, and his fondness for people hadn't changed a bit. All the hours he had spent with them, in training and on rides – thousands of kilometers of trail – had only made him enjoy their company more.

This was another light race year for Fosta. He was ridden regularly, often beside younger horses to teach them manners and give support, as they learned the tricks of the trail. He was fit and active, but the younger horses were taking the tests now, and Fosta, more often than not, stayed home.

The months went by, and it looked as though Fosta's race days were coming to a close, but when the call for

St. Albans came, the Lindsays could not ignore it. Of all the many tests they had taken together, they knew that Shahzada was Fosta's race. Fosta came to life on those trails. He knew every treacherous hill, every dangerous twist and turn, and most of all, *they* knew that he could do it again. *And* that he'd want to do it.

Helen and Alan both had horses chosen for the test already, so they offered Foz to Louise McCormack, as she was, once again, without a partner for the event.

There was a small field for Shahzada that year, with only eighty teams entered. The 1996 winner, Robert Ward, on his impressive mount, Hawkesbury Impala, was out to repeat his previous year's accomplishment, and was going after the speed record while he was at it. With a huge team of dedicated strappers waiting for them at the vet stops, he was setting the fastest pace ever seen at Shahzada, and it was decided early on that Louise and Fosta should avoid that pack and run their own race.

Fosta seemed happy to be back, and went to work on the challenging trails in his usual steady, sure-footed, confident way. In any other year, his effort would likely have earned him a top ten placing, but the front-runners were peeling hours off the usual average finishing time, and the Lindsays refused to push the aged gelding that five days and 40.41 hours on

– a full

sound

some record breaking of

1998 found Fosta living the easy life

training lightly with the younger horses, playing babysitter to the Lindsay youngsters, racing very little, and spending his days with his old pal, Bindo. But training picked up as the season wore on, and it was soon obvious that the Lindsays had something in mind for their old friend. Foz would not miss out on the trip to St. Albans that year, and Alan would not miss out on the chance to ride the old horse in his most important Shahzada effort of all.

Many a good horse had completed the Shahzada since it's inception seventeen years earlier, and several had done it more than once, but only a handful had shown the kind of consistency, soundness, and endurance that would lead to multiple completions.

One excellent horse named Gilgelad had topped the charts a few years earlier with ten completions out of twelve attempts. No other horse was even close to this record – except one little bay gelding with a heart as big as a house. If he could complete this test one more time, he would hold the record for the most completions in the fewest attempts – ten out of eleven – and he would set himself apart as a truly outstanding horse in the sport of endurance.

Throughout July and August, Alan worked with Fosta, preparing him for the job ahead. An older horse's body takes a little longer to get into hard condition, and there would be no "tightener" this year before Shahzada, so they had to prepare carefully.

When Foz stepped off the trailer in St. Albans that final week of September, he was in fine form and ready for the week ahead.

Robert Ward and Hawkesbury Impala were in full swing for the third year running, and once again would set a grueling pace. As usual, Alan rode competitively, but never pushed beyond what he thought his horse could do.

Fosta came to life under his old, familiar rider. Alan had always brought out the best in him, and this week, they were a team to be reckoned with. Foz was managing the hills and obstacles like the seasoned pro he was, and Alan was helping all he could.

... they had worked up to fifth

... eventual

...

muscles, and they were ...

attacking the hills and enjoying the bush tracks ...
had done for the past ten years together.

At times they were alone on the track, and the feeling was glorious – just the two of them, trotting through the early hours, the world awakening and unfolding from its sleep all around them. These were the moments Alan loved the most. The connection between a man and his horse could happen anywhere, but here, in these private moments, it was a connection almost beyond words.

At other times, they would come across competing teams, often riding in small, social packs. Some of the horses were there for the whole week event, while others were there for one of the forty-kilometer training rides that were incorporated into the bigger test to give young horses and less experienced riders the chance to experience the challenges of Shahzada without having to do the whole week.

It was one of these training ride teams that Alan and Foz came upon at one of the hills that morning. They had managed the steep incline in good time, and were beginning the difficult decline, when the younger horse became excited. Foz tried to avoid him, but the youngster kicked out behind him, catching Fosta square on the nose. By the time they reached the bottom, Foz was bleeding profusely and they had to stop.

Within a few minutes, the bleeding slowed, and eventually stopped, but when they hit the trail again, it was with a swollen nose and slightly impeded airway. Fosta got back to work as gamely as any horse could, but they had lost time, and were forced to go more slowly.

After a night of good care and rest, Fosta made his way onto the Shahzada trail for the last time Friday morning. His swelling had subsided and nothing was slowing his progress. He and Alan fairly flew over the demanding course that day, both reveling in the sport and the day that was theirs. Fosta's dark red coat gleamed in the Australian sunshine, and his dark little hooves danced over the ground he knew so well. It was the last time he would take a four-hundred-kilometer test, but he had nothing more to prove.

At the end of the day, he finished, once more, in the top ten, having completed the course in 34.05 hours – an excellent time for an old trooper! At the completion of [illegible] over eight thou- [illegible]

buckle, along with a large bronze [illegible] amazing achievement.

The little bay gelding, orphaned at birth, considered too small to amount to much, limited by his fears, and nearly defeated by a snake, stood quietly that day, unaware of just how outstanding he was. What he knew was that he was surrounded by the people he loved, being praised for doing the work he loved to do. And, that it was time to go home and rest.

10

The Rest

Fosta completed two more rides that year before being challenged in a new way by a condition known as stringhalts. Australian stringhalts, thought to be caused by certain toxins in plants, such as dandelions, causes exaggerated flexion of the hind legs when the horse tries to walk. In severely affected horses, walking becomes extremely difficult, as the hind legs are pulled violently up to the belly, causing the horse to bunny hop, and use it's front legs far more than usual. Fosta was very severely affected.

For over six months, Fosta struggled around a small [illegible] treatment sug- [illegible]

[illegible] pull him through. Helen put [illegible] together for company, and Bindo continuously bullied Foz into moving, keeping him from seizing up, and beginning the long process of repairing and strengthening the affected nerves and muscles. The positive effects of this forced exercise were noticed within a week or two of putting the geldings together, and within a few more months, Fosta was able to walk almost normally again. It would take longer yet for him to be able to trot, but he was finally on the road to recovery.

Ever so slowly, Fosta regained his strength and his old spark. He was soon teaching the youngest Lindsay to ride, and he and Erica formed a close bond that took them through years of Pony Club, several endurance tests, and many happy moments at Kintamani Stud.

Helen and Alan continued to use him to train young endurance horses, with the strong belief that complete retirement is the wrong thing to do with older, competitive horses. They may not be able to compete anymore, but they still love the trails, the attention, and the company.

At the age of twenty-five, Fosta traveled one last time to St. Albans. The Lindsays were taking a young horse for a training ride and thought maybe Foz would like to go again, just for fun. Fosta was right at home on the trails he knew so well, teaching the youngster he accompanied the rigors of the Shahzada test. Helen swore she saw a smile on his face when they were heading in toward base camp at the end of the half-day ride.

Fosta still lives at Kintamani Stud, carrying children around the Pony Club courses and hanging out with his old buddy, Bindo, who himself achieved over eleven thousand, five hundred kilometers before retiring. Fosta's amazing Shahzada record has yet to be broken, and he is as well loved, and as loving, as ever.

About the Author

Judy Andrekson grew up in Nova Scotia with a pen in one hand and a lead rope in the other. At the age of twenty, she moved to Alberta, where she could pursue her great love of horses, and there she worked for six years, managing a thoroughbred racehorse farm. By her thirties, Judy had also begun to write seriously. Now she combines both of her passions in her new series for young readers, True HORSE Stories. Judy also works as an educational assistant. She, her husband, and their daughter live in Sherwood Park, Alberta, with a constantly changing assortment of animals.

Praise for True HORSE Stories

"Sherwood Park author Judy Andrekson's characters dance, prance and bow in this new series of children's books called True Horse Stories.

Andrekson clearly understands and loves horses. . . . What makes these books unique in the large 'horse genre' of literature is that the stories are based on actual, non-fictional accounts of horses from around the world."

– *Strathcona County This Week*

"Short and easy to read, but with lots of impact, these . . . books are highly recommended."

– *Resource Links* **Rating: Excellent**

"If you know a young horse lover, this is the series for them. . . . Andrekson tells a story of a friendship between animal and human, where each partner benefits from the loyalty of the other. It is a fine message to share with young readers." – *The Chronicle Herald*

Little Squire: The Jumping Pony

Miskeen: The Dancing Horse

"It was *Miskeen: The Dancing Horse* that really sent me galloping back to the wholly imaginary paddock of my childhood. . . . Andrekson really engages the storytelling heart of her material . . . with a high degree of emotional engagement, complicated relationships and issues, and a well-realized personality."

– *Quill and Quire* **Featured Review**

JB Andrew: Mustang Magic

"This is a gripping story, full of tension and real life descriptions. . . . Judy Andrekson's knowledge and love of horses is very apparent. Her writing style is simple for young readers, but any adult who might choose to read the books in this series as family read-alouds will not be bored. They are fast-paced and full of action. . . . David Parkins' illustrations are wonderful. The personalities of the horse and his trainers shine brightly in each picture. . . . I would highly recommended this book to emerging readers, horse lovers or not."

– *Canadian Review of Materials*

Highly Recommended

Little Squire: The Jumping Pony
Miskeen: The Dancing Horse
JB Andrew: Mustang Magic
Fosta: Marathon Master
Brigadier: Gentle Hero